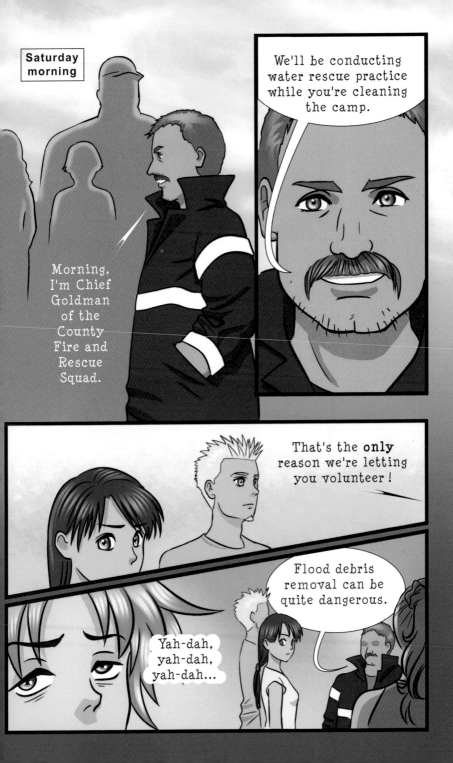

The firemen are setting up downstream. We're going to remove debris upstream.

Can I tag along with you guys?

Okay --

Oh, God, please save me.

SPLOOt!

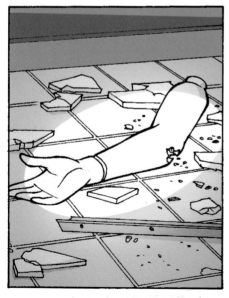

DRRNR
DRRNR
DWOOM
DWOOM

ANOTHER
AFTER-
SHOCK?

NO...
THUNDER?

BDWOOOOM

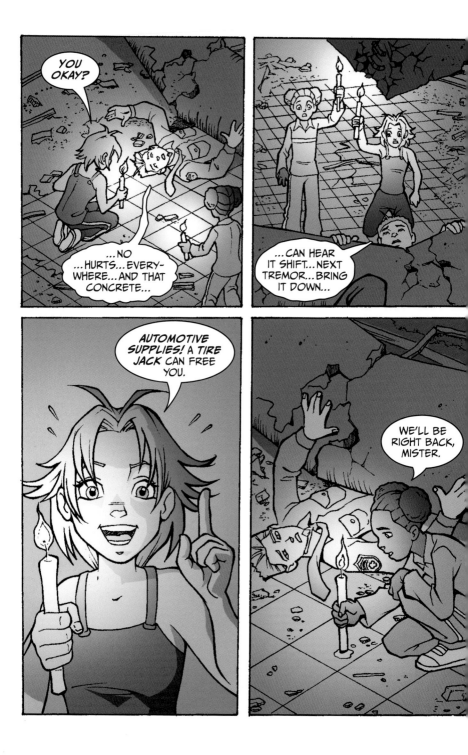

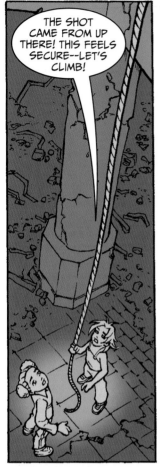

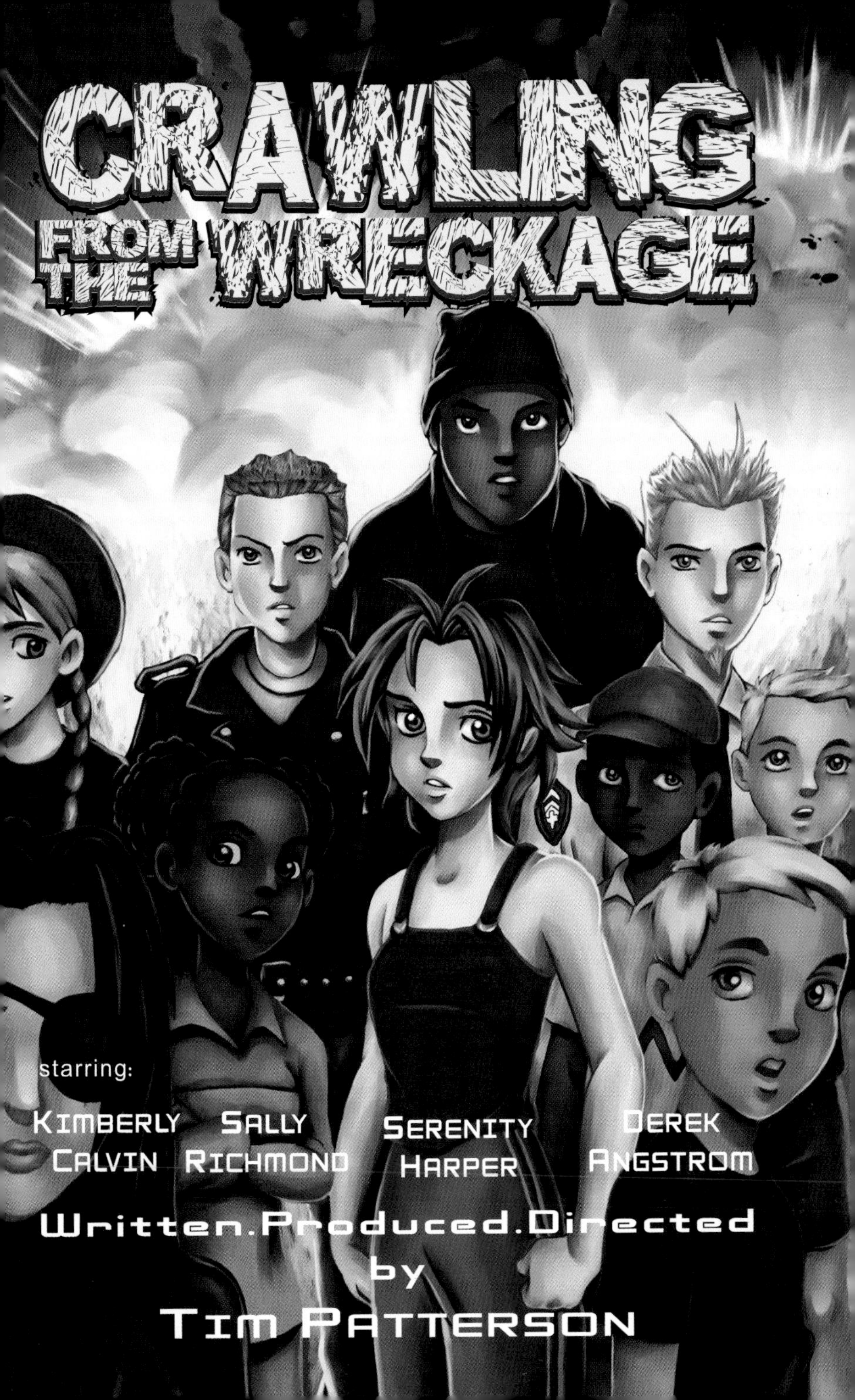

CRAWLING FROM THE WRECKAGE
starring:
KIMBERLY CALVIN
SALLY RICHMOND
SERENITY HARPER
DEREK ANGSTROM
Written.Produced.Directed by
TIM PATTERSON

How We Made

"CRAWLING FROM THE WRECKAGE"

by

Serenity Harper (Class 6a)

Guys get these crazy ideas (no, I'm not talking about THOSE ~~kinda~~ *kind of* crazy ideas). Tim said when he was a kid he used to fantasize about being the only survivor after a nuclear war and having all the toy stores to himself. He was one weird 6 year old if you ask me.

Anywho, he ~~axed~~ *asked* me about earthquakes and stuff. ~~and~~ then he came up with this idea for a disaster movie where Kimberly would be looking for her kid brothers in a wrecked mall only Kimberly didn't want to do that. ~~and~~ I was supposed to be the bad guy but when Kimberly heard I was supposed to smack her kid brothers around it was like "Hey! I ~~wanna~~ *want a* piece of that" so Tim let her be the bad girl and I got to be the good girl. Shouldn't this be "she said," ?

Talk about casting against type!

Anyway, K. had a great time smacking her kid bros around (are you paying attention, Derek? That's how she's ~~gonna~~ *going to* treat you one of these days!).

We shot one scene where the basement of the mall was supposed to be flooded so we got an old wading pool Sally's folks had. ~~and We~~ painted some carboard to look like a wrecked building. ~~and~~ I had to sit in it to pretend it was deep. Then I hadta dunk under and it was COLD!!! ~~'cuz~~ we was shooting at night ~~'cuz~~ the power because was supposed to be out in the mall. had to

Good newz: I got to rescue DEREK!!! and from Kimberly!!! Ha-ha!

Too many exclamaition points!

C-ya!

C-ren

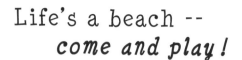

IT'S

LIFE !
CAMERA !
ACTION !
starring
Serenity™

Serenity is back with **ALL NEW STORIES** that mix humor, heartache, homework & just a touch of Hollywood hoopla as she and her friends start making their own brand of off-beat movies!

ALL THE SASS & TWICE THE **FUN!**

Don't miss these great new titles from Thomas Nelson & Realbuzz Studios!

"Space Cadet vs. Drama Queen"
"Sunday Best"
"Choosing Change"
"Girl Overboard"

MAKE THE JUMP TO OUR WEBSITES !

www.SerenityBuzz.com
www.GoofyfootGurl.com
and
www.RealbuzzStudios.com not only talk about
Serenity and the Prayer Club but also upcoming new
series from Thomas Nelson and Realbuzz Studios like
GOOFYFOOT GURL and many, **many more !**

Make sure you visit us regularly
for advance news, fun facts, downloads, contests
and challenges, as well as online shopping !

Can you make a video ?
Do you have a recipe ?

Exciting new contests
coming soon to
www.RealbuzzStudios.com !

Looking For

Serenity tm **Swag**

Or

Goofyfoot tm **Gear ?**

Serenity

Serenity

Created by Realbuzz Studios, Inc.
Min Kwon, Primary Artist

Serenity throws a big wet sloppy one out to:
Scott S. & his hard workin' crew, and to Peter G.

Smack!
Luv U Guyz !!!

©&TM 2007 by Realbuzz Studios   ISBN 1-59554-395-3 / 978-1-59554-395-0
www.RealbuzzStudios.com
www.SerenityBuzz.com

Published by Thomas Nelson, Inc. Nashville, TN 37214 www.thomasnelson.com

Library of Congress Cataloguing-in-Publication Data
Applied For

Scripture quotations marked NCV are taken from
The Holy Bible, New Century Version®. NCV®.
Copyright © 2001 by Nelson Bibles.
Used by permission of Thomas Nelson. All rights reserved.

Printed in Singapore.
5 4 3 2 1